Let's Look at Pumpkins

Katie Peters

GRL Consultants,
Diane Craig and Monica Marx,
Certified Literacy Specialists

Pull Ahead Readers

Lerner Publications ◆ Minneapolis

Note from a GRL Consultant
This Pull Ahead leveled book has been carefully designed for beginning readers. A team of guided reading literacy experts has reviewed and leveled the book to ensure readers pull ahead and experience success.

Lerner Publications Company
An imprint of Lerner Publishing Group, Inc.
241 First Avenue North
Minneapolis, MN 55401 USA

For reading levels and more information, look up this title at www.lernerbooks.com.

Main body text set in Memphis Pro 24/39
Typeface provided by Linotype.

Photo Acknowledgments
The images in this book are used with the permission of: © Jodi Jacobson/iStockphoto, pp. 14, 15, 16 (pumpkins); © Ibrix/iStockphoto, pp. 10, 11, 16 (flower); © LightFieldStudios/iStockphoto, pp. 4, 5, 16 (seed); © PatrikStedrak/iStockphoto, pp. 8, 9, 16 (vine); © saiko3p/iStockphoto, pp. 6, 7; © skodonnell/iStockphoto, p. 3; © zorazhuang/iStockphoto, pp. 12, 13.

Front cover: © Holly Cromer/iStockphoto

Library of Congress Cataloging-in-Publication Data

Names: Peters, Katie, author.
Title: Let's look at pumpkins / Katie Peters.
Description: Minneapolis : Lerner Publications, [2021] | Series: Plant life cycles (pull ahead readers - nonfiction) | Includes index. | Audience: Ages 4–7 | Audience: Grades K–1 | Summary: "How do small, flat pumpkin seeds become large, round pumpkins? This title uses carefully leveled text and vibrant photos to show younger readers exactly how. Pairs with the fiction title Pumpkin Seeds."— Provided by publisher.
Identifiers: LCCN 2019046323 (print) | LCCN 2019046324 (ebook) | ISBN 9781541590212 (library binding) | ISBN 9781728403144 (paperback) | ISBN 9781728400761 (ebook)
Subjects: LCSH: Pumpkin—Life cycles—Juvenile literature.
Classification: LCC SB347 .P435 2021 (print) | LCC SB347 (ebook) | DDC 635/.62—dc23

LC record available at https://lccn.loc.gov/2019046323
LC ebook record available at https://lccn.loc.gov/2019046324

Manufactured in the United States of America
4-1011168-48075-11/11/2024

Contents

Let's Look at Pumpkins

Pumpkin seeds are flat.
I plant the seeds in dirt.

The seeds need water.
The seeds need sun.
They start to grow.

Long vines grow.

Leaves grow on the vines.

Flowers grow on the vines.
The flowers are yellow.

Pumpkins grow on the vines.
The pumpkins are green.

The pumpkins grow bigger. They turn orange. It is time to pick the pumpkins!

Did You See It?

pumpkin flower

pumpkins

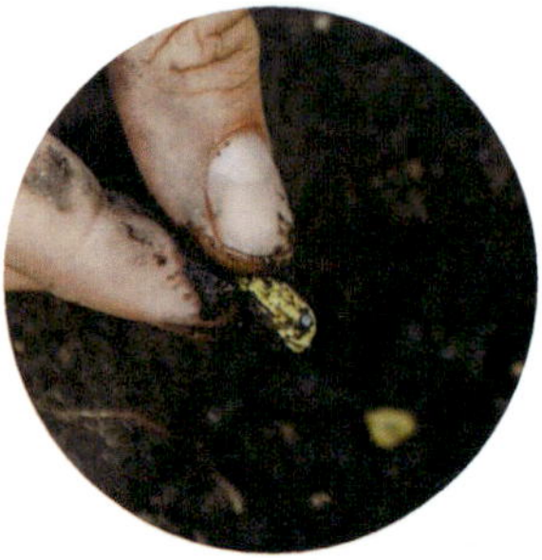

pumpkin seeds

pumpkin vine

Index